Samantha's
Short Story
Collection

BELONGS TO

Elizabeth

Makris

_____

DATE

Read all of the novels about Samantha:

The adventures of *Samantha Parkington* continue in this keepsake collection of short stories. Samantha's growing up with her wealthy grandmother at the beginning of the twentieth century. New inventions and ideas are making Samantha's world even more exciting. But not everyone's life is changing for the better. Samantha's generous spirit and willingness to speak up help her shape her own idea of what progress means in America.

Discover more about Samantha's world in these heartwarming stories of new ideas and unfailing compassion.

Samantha's
SHORT STORY
COLLECTION

By VALERIE TRIPP AND
SARAH MASTERS BUCKEY

ILLUSTRATIONS BY DAN ANDREASEN AND
TROY HOWELL

VIGNETTES BY SUSAN MCALILEY AND
PHILIP HOOD

Published by Pleasant Company Publications
Copyright © 2006 by American Girl, LLC
All rights reserved. No part of this book may be used or reproduced in
any manner whatsoever without written permission except in the case of
brief quotations embodied in critical articles and reviews.

Questions or comments? Call 1-800-845-0005,
visit our Web site at **americangirl.com**, or write to Customer Service,
American Girl, 8400 Fairway Place, Middleton, WI 53562-0497.

Printed in China
06 07 08 09 10 11 LEO 12 11 10 9 8 7 6 5 4 3 2 1

American Girl™ and its associated logos, Samantha®,
and Samantha Parkington® are trademarks of American Girl, LLC.

Cataloging-in-Publication Data
available from the Library of Congress.

PICTURE CREDITS

TABLE OF CONTENTS
SAMANTHA'S FAMILY
AND FRIENDS

❧

SAMANTHA'S FAMILY

GRANDMARY
*Samantha's grandmother, who
wants her to be a young lady*

UNCLE GARD
*Samantha's favorite uncle,
who calls her Sam*

SAMANTHA
*An orphan who lives
with her wealthy
grandmother*

CORNELIA
*An old-fashioned beauty who
has newfangled ideas*

NELLIE
*Samantha's friend who works
as a maid*

AGNES AND AGATHA
*Samantha's newest friends,
who are Cornelia's sisters*

ALICE
*Cornelia's youngest sister,
who is three years old*

SAMANTHA'S FRIENDS

MRS. VAN SICKLEN
*Grandmary's neighbor and
Nellie's boss*

IDA
*Samantha's school friend, who
is the best artist in the class*

EDDIE
*Samantha's neighbor, who
loves to tease*

MARGUERITE
*A shy but talented girl who
just arrived from France*

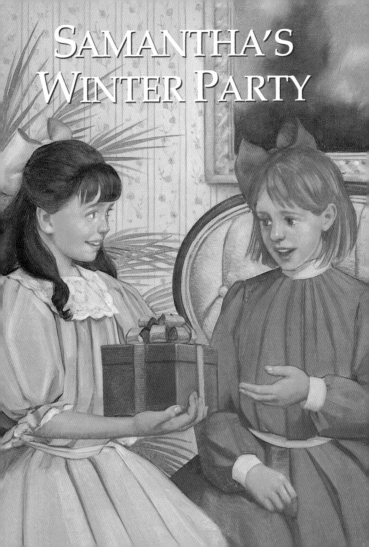

SAMANTHA'S WINTER PARTY

Let's race!" Samantha called. Across Culpepper's Pond she skated, going so fast she felt as if she were flying. Ida, Helen, Ruth, and Nellie were right behind her, their skates flashing. The race ended in a tie as all five girls skidded up to the edge of the pond at the same time. They collapsed on the bench together in a breathless, giggling heap.

"Jeepers!" said Ida after they'd untangled themselves. "My fingers are so

stiff I can hardly undo my skates!"

"I hope it stays this cold," said
Samantha. "Won't it be fun to skate
during our Christmas vacation?"

"Oh, yes!" The other girls agreed
happily.

It had been the coldest winter anyone could remember. For weeks now,

Culpepper's Pond had been frozen solid.
Skating was all the rage. Almost every day,
Samantha, Ida, Helen, and Ruth burst out
of Miss Crampton's Academy with their
schoolbooks under their arms and their
ice skates slung over their shoulders and
rushed straight to the pond.

This Friday afternoon skating was
especially fun because Samantha's friend
Nellie was able to come, too. Nellie was
a good skater. She was teaching the others
how to skate backward and do figure
eights. All the girls liked it when Nellie
came to the pond, but she could only come
on Mondays and Fridays. Nellie and her
parents were servants for Mrs. Van Sicklen,
and Nellie usually had to work.

Samantha looked out at the crowd as she unbuckled her skates. In their bright hats and coats, the skaters looked like a flock of colorful birds, swooping, skimming, and swirling across the ice. Two of the skaters left the crowd and skated toward the bench. Samantha saw that they were Edith and Clarisse, who also went to Miss Crampton's Academy. "Hello," Samantha said politely as the girls stopped.

But Edith didn't waste time with politeness. "I'm having a party Monday after school, and my mother is making me invite all the girls in my class at Miss Crampton's," she said. "So that means all of you—except

Nellie, of course—have to come. We're
going to practice our song for the
Christmas pageant."

"Monday?" asked Samantha.

Helen blurted out what Samantha
was thinking: "But that means we'll miss
skating with Nellie!"

Edith sniffed. "Well, then, you needn't
stay at the party very long. That way
you'll have time to skate with your friend
the servant girl."

Clarisse had been staring at Nellie's
skates. They were very old, and the blades
and buckles were rusty. Now
Clarisse whispered some-
thing to Edith, and they both
smirked. As they skated away,

Clarisse said in a loud voice, "I think it's pathetic the way that Nellie is always trying to keep up with her betters!"

Nellie quickly bent down to gather up her schoolbooks, but Samantha could see that her cheeks were red. Samantha was so angry at Edith and Clarisse for hurting Nellie's feelings she wished she could punch them! "Don't pay any attention to those nincompoops, Nellie," she said.

"That's right," said Helen. She crossed her eyes and stuck her tongue out at the girls' backs.

"I wish I didn't have to go to Edith's party," said Ida. "It won't be fun."

"I know!" said Samantha, with enthusiasm. "Let's have our own special party next Friday!"

"Oh, yes, let's!" agreed Helen and
Ida and Ruth.

"We'll skate first, and then we can
have the party at my house," said
Samantha. "I'm sure Grandmary
will allow it. We can sing carols
and eat cookies and drink cocoa—"

"And we can give each other
presents!" Helen piped up. "Special
presents for our most special friends."

"Yes!" agreed all the girls—all except
Nellie.

Nellie was very quiet. Immediately,
Samantha realized why. *Nellie has no
money. She cannot possibly buy presents for
us*, she thought. *Oh dear! I brought up the*

party to make Nellie feel better, and now I'm afraid it's made her feel worse!

Samantha thought hard as Ida, Helen, and Ruth chattered on about the party and joked about the presents they were going to give each other. After the other girls said good-bye and headed home, Samantha smiled at her friend.

"Nellie, I have a good idea!" she said. "Why don't you and I get together and *make* presents for the other girls? Wouldn't that be fun?"

Nellie looked uncertain. "Do you think homemade presents will be all right?" she asked. "All the other girls will have store-bought."

"Good gifts don't have to cost

money!" said Samantha. "Once I saw someone make really nice Christmas corsages out of pinecones."

"Corsages!" said Nellie. "That's so grown-up! Do you remember how to make them?"

"I think so," said Samantha. "Anyway, how hard can it be? Let's meet tomorrow afternoon and collect a lot of pinecones."

Nellie smiled. "I'll bring a basket," she said.

❧

A light snow was falling the next afternoon as Samantha and Nellie walked through the woods just behind the Van Sicklens' house, filling Nellie's basket with pinecones.

"Be careful where you step," Nellie warned Samantha. "It's marshy. There are puddles as big as small ponds in here."

Samantha scraped a bit of the snow away with the toe of her boot. "The puddles are all frozen," she said. "See? There's ice under the snow." She looked around. "It's pretty here, isn't it?"

"Pretty and *cold*," said Nellie, shivering. "Let's go inside."

The girls hurried to Samantha's house. It was cozy in the kitchen. On the table, Samantha had carefully set out everything they needed to make their corsages. They began eagerly, talking as they worked.

"The other girls are going to be so pleased that we made our presents for them all by ourselves," said Samantha.

"It will be a surprise!" said Nellie happily.

But making the corsages was a lot harder than Samantha had remembered. The gold paint was globby. The cheery sprigs of holly pricked their fingers. The Christmas-red ribbon wouldn't stay tied in bows. The lacy paper snowflakes refused to stick on the pinecones. Samantha and Nellie grew quieter and quieter as they became more and more discouraged.

After hours of struggle, the kitchen table was sticky with glue and globs of gold paint. It was littered with short bits of ribbon, crushed holly sprigs, and clumps of wadded-up paper. Samantha wrinkled her brow and held up a mangled-looking, splotchy, gluey pine-cone. "I must have forgotten some important step," she said. "This doesn't look anything like a corsage."

"Mine doesn't, either," Nellie said. She sighed. "The corsages were a nice idea, Samantha," she went on kindly. "But let's be honest. They're not working."

"What if we put jingle bells on them?" asked Samantha. "I've got some we could use."

But Nellie shook her head and grinned a little. "We'd need something more than jingle bells to make these look

any good," she said. "We'd need something *magic.*"

"You're right," Samantha admitted. "We might as well throw this stuff away."

In silence, the girls swept the crumpled paper, wrinkled ribbons, and globby gold pinecones off the table and into Nellie's basket. "Maybe we could try making something else for the girls," Samantha suggested at last. "Or maybe we could *find* something—"

"No," Nellie said firmly. "I know you're trying to help me, Samantha, but you can't." She tossed a pinecone into the basket and dusted off her hands. "Clarisse was right," she said. "Servant girls shouldn't try to 'keep up.' I don't have any money to spend the way you and your friends do."

Samantha felt helpless. "But you'll come to the party on Friday, won't you, Nellie?" she asked. "The party will be the most fun. Presents don't matter. No one expects . . . I mean, no one will care if you don't give—"

Nellie interrupted. "*I* would care," she said simply. She picked up the basket of scraps. "I'll get rid of this," she said. And then she left.

Samantha slumped at the table. She had hurt Nellie's pride. Now Nellie might not come to the party. It seemed the more Samantha tried to make things better, the more she made things worse.

❧

Samantha, Helen, Ruth, and Ida had rushed to the pond after Edith's party on Monday, but they could not find Nellie. No one had seen her skating that afternoon.

"Gosh!" said Ruth. "Why isn't Nellie here? She knew we were coming. She's never missed a Monday afternoon before!"

"I sure hope she comes Friday," said Helen. "The party won't be fun without her."

Samantha said nothing. She knew why Nellie wasn't there. *She's avoiding us,* Samantha thought. *Oh, I've got to talk to her!*

After skating, Samantha went straight to the Van Sicklens' house and knocked on the front door. Nellie's father opened it. "Why, hello, Samantha," he said. "How may I help you today?"

"Please, Mr. O'Malley," said Samantha. "May I see Nellie?"

Mr. O'Malley seemed to hesitate, but

then he smiled. "Come in and wait in the hall," he said.

"Thank you," said Samantha. As she stood waiting, she could hear Mr. O'Malley talking to Nellie in the kitchen.

"Samantha's here," he said.

"Oh, no!" Samantha heard Nellie say.

Samantha's heart sank. Nellie didn't want to see her!

When Nellie appeared, she seemed nervous. "Hello, Samantha," she said.

"Nellie, we missed you at the pond," said Samantha.

"Oh!" said Nellie. "I . . . I was busy."

Samantha had never seen Nellie so stiff and unfriendly! "Oh, Nellie," she burst out. "Can't we go into the kitchen

Samantha had never seen Nellie so stiff and unfriendly!

and talk for a while?"

"No!" said Nellie quickly. "We can't. I . . . uh, I'd better get back to work." She opened the front door. "Thank you for coming, Samantha. You'd better go now."

Before Samantha knew it, she was back outside. Even more bitter than the cold was the feeling that she had lost her friend. There could be no doubt about it— Nellie did not want to see Samantha or talk to her. Samantha trudged home sadly.

The day of the party was dreary and cold. After school, when the girls got to Culpepper's Pond, Samantha was sorry but not surprised to see that Nellie was not there. The girls skated without her, but after a while Helen said, "Maybe Nellie's waiting for us at your house, Samantha. Shall we go see?"

They walked up the hill, dropped their skates in a pile on the front porch, and filed inside.

Nellie wasn't there.

"Well," said Samantha glumly. "We might as well have some refreshments."

As the girls were getting their first cups of cocoa, Nellie appeared at the door to the parlor. She had a big red bow in her hair and a big smile on her face.

"Nellie!" the girls cried in delight as they rushed to her. "You're here!"

"Oh, we were so afraid you weren't coming!" said Ida.

"Now that you've come, the party can begin!" said Helen.

Samantha was too relieved and delighted to say anything. She sat at the piano and played "The Twelve Days of Christmas" as loudly as she could. The girls got the words all mixed up. No one could remember if it was the lords who were leaping or the ladies, but no one seemed to mind. And Ruth sang "five goooolden rings" in such a funny, warbling voice that they all collapsed with laughter. Singing made them hungry, so they ate cookies and drank more steaming cups of cocoa beside the fire.

"Now!" said Ida, setting down her empty cup. "Let's open our presents."

Samantha watched Nellie carefully out of the corner of her eye. Nellie hadn't brought any packages, but she watched her friends exchange gifts with happy, glowing eyes.

"Here, Nellie," said Samantha, handing her a big box. "We all chipped in to buy this gift for you."

"Thank you," said Nellie politely. She opened the box, and her face grew pink. "Oh, *thank you!*" she said again

 as she lifted out a beautiful pair of ice skates. "What a wonderful surprise!"

Then suddenly Nellie

"Here, Nellie," said Samantha, handing her a big box.
"We all chipped in to buy this gift for you."

stood up, and holding her skates to her chest, she said, "Now you must all get your skates and come with me, because I have a surprise for *you*."

Giggling and chattering, the girls put on their coats. They followed Nellie out the door and picked up their skates on the porch. The sun was just setting. The sky was dark purple streaked with pink, and a few early stars were out. Nellie led the curious and excited girls through the twilight to the woods behind the Van Sicklens' house. When at last she stopped among the trees, her friends all gasped in amazement at what they saw.

"Ooooooh!" they sighed.

The woods were transformed! Nellie

had swept the snow off the ice so that all the small, perfect ponds were clear. One pond led to another, like shiny stepping stones made of mirrors. The ponds were rimmed by candles planted in the snow and by small bouquets of holly sprigs. Nellie had hung lanterns from the largest tree branches, and their light glowed against the wintry dusk. Glittering gold pinecones and lacy paper snowflakes hung from the trees, too, and bits of red ribbon fluttered and danced.

"It's like an enchanted forest," whispered Samantha, and all the girls murmured in agreement.

At that moment, Mr. O'Malley

"It's like an enchanted forest," whispered Samantha,
and all the girls murmured in agreement.

26

appeared, carrying his violin. As the girls strapped on their skates, he began to play a waltz, and the thin notes floated clear and fine on the night air.

Samantha skated next to Nellie. "It's so beautiful, Nellie!" she said.

Nellie beamed. "My dad helped me," she said. "We came out here together early this morning, before sunrise. He checked the ice to be sure it was safe, and he helped me put up the decorations, too. But it was my idea! I made the decorations out of the scraps from our corsage project. I was making them the day you came to see me, Samantha, and that's why I couldn't let you come into the kitchen. I wanted my gift for you to be a surprise!"

"It's the most wonderful surprise I've ever seen!" said Samantha. "I don't know how you ever did it."

Nellie smiled and twirled in a little circle on the ice. "Oh," she said. "It was just a little magic."

Looking Back

Ice-Skating
in 1904

Skating costumes made it hard to jump and spin.

When Samantha was growing up, ice-skating was all the rage. People loved to strap on their skates and show off their fancy footwork. And it was some-thing almost every-one could do—all they needed was a pair of skates and a frozen lake or pond. People who weren't

A skate chair in Central Park

good skaters could sit in skate chairs and be pushed across the ice.

People have skated for thousands of years. The earliest known skate, made of animal bone, is said to be more than two thousand years old! Skating became much easier as skates were made of wood, iron, and finally steel in the early 1800s. These early skates had straps that buckled around a skater's shoes or boots. The skaters moved stiffly because they didn't want their shoes or boots to slip out of the skates. They concentrated on carving complicated patterns such as the "rattlesnake" or a "rosette" with their sharp blades. One skater even etched an entire love letter to his sweetheart in the ice!

Rattlesnake

In 1850 a strapless skate was invented. It had blades that clipped right into the boot. Now skaters could twist, turn, spin, and leap without losing their blades. Over the next few years, lots of changes were made in skate design. The front of the blade changed from a curve to a sharp point. This let skaters perform fancier moves. Skates with *toe picks,* or sharp teeth in the front

of the blade, also appeared. Toe picks helped skaters with jumps and spins. Around the turn of the century,

This ladies' skate cost $2.38 in 1902.

skates like those we have today, with the blade and the boot attached as one piece, were invented.

In New York City, many people skated on the lake in Central Park. When the park was built, it attracted almost forty thousand skaters every day. New

Ice-skating in Central Park became popular in the 1850s.

Yorkers knew the lake was safe to skate on when a red ball was up in the bell tower next to the lake.

In the 1890s, an indoor ice rink called Empire City was built in New York. It was the size of a football field. The rink had music playing and was lit with gaslights so skaters could skate at night.

When people skated at night in the

Empire City

country, they carried a skater's lamp. The lamp had a chain with a ring that hooked onto a skater's finger. The light helped skaters avoid obstacles on the ice like sticks, rough spots, and other people!

A skater's lamp

Around 1900, women began to compete in ice-skating. One of the first was Madge Syers of Great Britain. She entered the all-male world championship in 1902. Madge defeated two men to place second in the competition! The next year, skating officials stopped women from competing against men because their long dresses

prevented judges from seeing their feet. In 1905 a separate ladies' championship was established, and Madge won in 1906 and 1907. A year later, she became the first female Olympic figure-skating gold medalist.

Madge Syers was the first great female skater.

At the 1920 Olympic Games, a judge warned American skater Theresa Weld that it was not proper for a woman to perform jumps because her skirt would fly up to her knees. If she did jump, she would lose points. Theresa didn't pay any attention to the judge and put a small jump in her program. She won her free-skating program and a bronze medal overall.

Then in 1924 figure skating was changed again, this time by an 11-year-old girl. At the Olympic Games, Sonja Henie wore a knee-length skirt, the style for a girl her age. The shorter skirt allowed her to spin and

Sonja was 6 years old when she got her first pair of skates.

37

jump like male skaters. At the time, jumps were not considered ladylike. The shocked judges gave Sonja last place!

Four years later, Sonja surprised the judges again by combining dance patterns and ice-skating. But this time the judges liked her new approach, and she took home the first of her ten world titles. Sonja began to be called the "Pavlova of the Ice" after her idol, ballerina Anna Pavlova. Sonja's programs encouraged all women skaters to

Sonja Henie at the St. Moritz Olympics in 1928

38

skate more athletic programs. Women began jumping and spinning as they never had before! By 1930, Sonja was everywhere—even in Hollywood movies. Her influence is still seen today. Since

Sonja didn't like black skates, she wore beige ones instead. When her competitors copied her, Sonja wore white skates. Most girls since then have worn white skates, too!

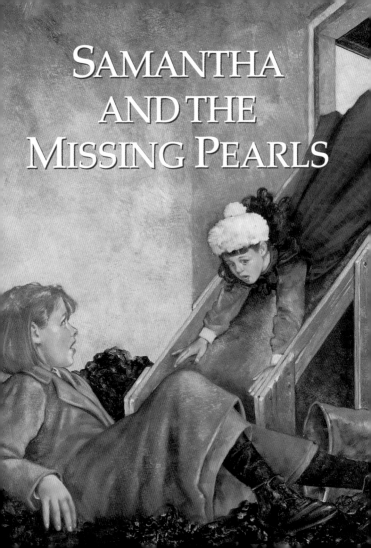

SAMANTHA
AND THE
MISSING PEARLS

SAMANTHA AND THE MISSING PEARLS

R un, Samantha, run!" cried Nellie. "The dog is right behind us!"

Hearts pounding, Samantha and Nellie dashed across the drive and up the steps to Mrs. Van Sicklen's back porch. They flung open the kitchen door and ran inside. Nellie slammed the door shut, making the Christmas wreath swing wildly. Outside they heard noisy barking and the clumsy scrabbling of huge paws on the wooden porch floor.

43

Samantha leaned against the door and gasped, "I hate that dog."

"Me, too," agreed Nellie. "He's just as mean as his owner, Jones."

Jones was the new hired man at Mrs. Van Sicklen's house. Nellie and her family also worked for the Van Sicklens, and Jones had a room in the carriage house next to theirs. Jones was not a friendly neighbor. He never smiled and hardly ever spoke except to growl, "Stay away from there!" or "Watch out for that!" Jones was a handyman. He also emptied the ash cans, so he was always covered with gray ash.

"Jones is as gray as a ghost," said Samantha.

"He's an old crosspatch,"
said Nellie. "Yesterday he
scolded me for cutting holly
branches. I needed them to make wreaths."

"Oh, Nellie!" said Samantha. "Can
you teach me to make a wreath?"

"Not right now," Nellie answered.
"Mrs. Van Sicklen is having a tea party
today, and I have to get everything ready.
My mother and father are away."

"I'll help!" said Samantha. "I love tea
parties. Who's coming?"

"Mrs. Eddleton and Mrs. Ryland,"
said Nellie.

Samantha made a face. "Oh dear
me! How perfectly dreadful!" she said,
imitating Mrs. Eddleton's shrill voice.

Mrs. Eddleton and Mrs. Ryland were hoity-toity ladies. They did not think Samantha and Nellie should be friends because Nellie was a servant and Samantha was a young lady.

Nellie grinned at Samantha's imitation, then turned to fill the kettle. "The ladies are going to give each other their Christmas presents," she said. "Mrs. Van Sicklen already opened the present her mother sent. You should see it, Samantha. It's a necklace of pearls. They're called black pearls, but they're really gray, a lovely dark—" Suddenly the girls heard a shout. "Nellie!" It was Mrs. Van Sicklen. "Nellie! Come quickly!" she cried.

Samantha and Nellie ran from the kitchen to the hallway and saw Mrs. Van Sicklen flying down the stairs. "They're gone!" she wailed. "My new black pearls! They've disappeared!"

"Oh, no!" gasped the girls.

Mrs. Van Sicklen's voice was shaky. "Those pearls are priceless!" she said.

"Mrs. Van Sicklen, ma'am, where did you last see the pearls?" Nellie asked.

"I put them on my dressing table last night," Mrs. Van Sicklen answered. "I've been in bed all day with a sick headache, so I didn't notice they were gone until just now. I was going to put them on to show the ladies at tea. But I've searched everywhere in my room, and they're gone!"

Before Nellie or Samantha could say another word, the doorbell rang. Nellie opened the door and there stood Mrs. Ryland and Mrs. Eddleton, their arms full of Christmas packages. When the ladies saw Mrs. Van Sicklen's face they both asked, "What's wrong?"

"You look so distressed, my dear!" said Mrs. Eddleton.

"My new black pearl necklace has disappeared!" said Mrs. Van Sicklen.

"You've been robbed! Call the police!" boomed Mrs. Ryland. She clutched her packages and looked all around as if the thief might be lurking nearby.

"Robbed! Oh dear me! How perfectly dreadful!" shrilled Mrs. Eddleton. She took Mrs. Van Sicklen by the elbow and led her toward the parlor.

"Do you really think . . ." Mrs. Van Sicklen began.

Mrs. Eddleton lowered her voice, but Samantha and Nellie both heard her say, "Of course! Didn't I tell you there'd be trouble when you hired that Nellie and her family to be servants?"

"But they were gone last night," said Mrs. Van Sicklen. "Well, all but Nellie."

"Nellie!" Mrs. Eddleton said as the parlor door closed behind her. "I never did trust that girl."

Samantha and Nellie looked at each other, horrified. "Oh, Nellie!" exclaimed Samantha. "They think *you* might have stolen the pearls! How dare they jump to that conclusion!"

Nellie's face was serious. "Samantha," she said quietly, "we've got to find those missing pearls. We've just got to."

"We will!" said Samantha firmly. "Let's go search Mrs. Van Sicklen's room.

Maybe she didn't look carefully enough."

Nellie led the way up the stairs and into Mrs. Van Sicklen's room. "When I came in this morning, Mrs. Van Sicklen was asleep," she explained. "I set her breakfast tray on the dressing table as usual. Then I swept the ashes from the fireplace into my ash scuttle, put coal on the grate, started a new fire, and took the ashes down to the cellar."

"Did you see the pearls on the dressing table?" asked Samantha.

"No," said Nellie, "but the room was dark. Let's search now."

The two girls searched through the powder puffs and perfume bottles, hairbrushes, hand mirrors, hankies, and hairpins on the dressing table. No pearls.

They crawled on their hands and knees to examine every inch of the floor. They wiggled under the bed, raked through the ashes in the fireplace, and even looked under the rug. No pearls.

"A thief must have come in last night when Mrs. Van Sicklen was asleep and stolen them," said Nellie.

"He probably planned this robbery very carefully," said Samantha.

"I don't think so," said Nellie. "Mrs. Van Sicklen got the necklace yesterday. No one saw it except me and . . ." Nellie stopped.

"Who?" asked Samantha.

"Jones!" said Nellie. "He was in the parlor fixing a chair when I brought Mrs. Van Sicklen the package. He saw her open it and take out the necklace."

"Jones!" exclaimed Samantha. "I bet *he* stole the pearls! Let's go search his room!"

"Oh, no, Samantha!" said Nellie. "I wouldn't dare! Besides, if Jones *did* steal the pearls, how did he get into the house last night? He doesn't have a key. And all the doors and windows are locked up tight."

"He could have broken a window to climb in," said Samantha. "Let's go search the outside of the house."

Samantha and Nellie crept down the stairs and past the parlor where the ladies were waiting for the police. Quickly, the girls put on their coats, peeked out the back door to be sure Jones was not around, and ran down the back steps. Just as they were coming around the corner of the house, Samantha saw Jones and his dog coming toward them across the drive. Instantly, Samantha drew back and held out her arm to stop Nellie until Jones and the dog had passed.

"Phew!" whispered Nellie in relief. "That was close!"

"Yes," said Samantha. "If Jones sees us searching the house, he may guess that we suspect him! Then he might do anything to stop us from proving he's the thief!"

The late December afternoon was

*Samantha drew back and held out her arm to stop
Nellie until Jones and the dog had passed.*

gloomy and raw. Samantha and Nellie searched every window and door for signs that someone had broken into the house, but they didn't find anything.

"I can't see the windows on the second and third floors very well," said Samantha. "We'll have to get a ladder, so I can get a better look."

"A ladder?" Nellie asked, shivering. They were standing next to the coal chute, feeling cold and discouraged. "You're going to climb up and look at every single window?"

"Well, I can't figure out how else Jones could have broken in," said Samantha.

"Me, either," said Nellie with a sigh.

She slumped back against the coal chute.

"Wait!" exclaimed Samantha. "The coal chute! It's never locked. Maybe Jones slid down the *chute* into the house."

"It's too narrow," said Nellie. "Jones could never fit in it."

Samantha pulled open the small trapdoor over the coal chute. "Let's see," she began.

But at that moment, Nellie and Samantha heard the clanking sound of the dog's collar. Both girls froze. Fear seemed to have fastened their feet to the ground.

"The dog," whispered Nellie, "and Jones! They're coming!"

"Quick!" said Samantha. "Hide!"

"But where?" asked Nellie.

Samantha looked around desperately. "Jump down the coal chute," she said.

"But . . ." Nellie protested.

"Go!" said Samantha, just as Jones and the dog rounded the corner and saw them. "Now!"

"Get away from there, you girls!" Jones yelled at them. But Nellie was already headed down the chute, with Samantha right behind her!

Swoosh! They slid down the short, steep chute. *Thud!* They landed on a pile of coal, making it spill out of the bin. The two girls rolled and tumbled to the cellar floor. Then *crash!* Their waving arms

Swoosh! *They slid down the short, steep chute.* **Thud!**
They landed on a pile of coal, making it spill out of the bin.

and legs knocked over ash cans that were filled to the brim. Ashes flew through the air like gray snow. The girls were coughing and choking when suddenly the cellar door swung open and all three ladies came thundering down the stairs.

"Good heavens!" gasped Mrs. Van Sicklen when she saw the girls sitting in the ashes. "What is going on here?"

Jones's gruff voice came from above, echoing down the coal chute. "They went and jumped down the chute, ma'am!" he announced. "Of all the fool things! Why, someone ought to . . ."

"That's enough, Jones!" said Mrs. Van Sicklen. They heard Jones slam shut the door to the chute with an angry *bang!*

"Girls," said Mrs. Van Sicklen. "How did you make this terrible mess?"

"Well," said Samantha. "Jones is right. We *did* jump down the coal chute."

"But *why?*" asked Mrs. Van Sicklen.

"We didn't mean any harm," said Samantha, glancing at Nellie as she struggled to her feet. Nellie didn't seem to be paying any attention. Instead she was looking intently at something in the ashes by her skirt. Samantha went on, "We were trying to find your necklace and—"

But Nellie interrupted her. "And we *did* find it!" she said triumphantly.

Samantha gasped. There in Nellie's sooty hand was the necklace. It was covered with ashes, but it was not broken. "Oh, Nellie!" exclaimed Samantha. She gave her friend a hug. Then Nellie handed the necklace to Mrs. Van Sicklen.

"Thank you, Nellie," said Mrs. Van Sicklen. She looked relieved but confused.

"*How* did my necklace get down *here?*"
she asked.

"It must have fallen off your dressing
table," said Nellie. "I must have swept
it up when I cleaned out your fireplace
this morning. I guess I didn't notice it
because the pearls are as gray as the
ashes. I scooped the ashes and the necklace into the scuttle, carried them down
here, and poured them into the ash can.
Then when Samantha and I knocked over
the cans, the necklace fell out. I found it
in the ashes when I tried to stand up."

"But," fussed Mrs. Ryland, "what
were you doing near the coal chute in
the first place, and why did you jump
down it?"

Samantha and Nellie looked at each other, shamefaced. "We were searching the house because we suspected Jo—I mean, we suspected a thief had broken in," said Samantha.

"You were not the only ones to suspect someone wrongly," said Mrs. Van Sicklen with a cool glance toward Mrs. Eddleton. "I'm proud of you girls and how you solved the mystery of my missing pearls. I can't imagine how you ever came to such a clever conclusion!"

"Well," said Samantha, grinning at Nellie, "you might say we *jumped* to that conclusion. But I don't think we'll jump to any more conclusions ever again. Do you, Nellie?"

"No," said Nellie, smiling. "Never again!"

LOOKING BACK

THE BOXCAR
CHILDREN

Gertrude (upper left), age 11, with Frances, John, and her parents

When Samantha was growing up in the early 1900s, Gertrude Chandler Warner, the creator of the Boxcar Children mystery series, was also growing up. Gertrude was born in 1890, and she lived right across the street from a railroad station.

From the time Gertrude was five years old, she wanted to become an author. When Gertrude was nine years old, she and her sister, Frances, wrote and illustrated their

first book. It was called *Golliwogg at the Zoo*, and they gave it to their grandfather for Christmas. Every year after that, Gertrude and her sister gave their grandparents a new book. They called their publishing company Warner & Co.

Gertrude also loved to read, and she often went to the public library to find books. Her favorite was *Alice's Adventures in Wonderland*. One Saturday morning, Gertrude checked out a book, read it, and returned it that same day. But she was disappointed when she couldn't take another book out on the same day—she had to wait until Wednesday, the next time the library opened!

Another pastime Gertrude enjoyed was making furniture for her dollhouse. In 1916 she turned this childhood love  into her first published book, called *The House of Delight*. It was about her childhood dollhouse, where the china dolls Mr. and Mrs. Delight lived.

Gertrude began teaching in 1918, but she kept writing stories. One day, Gertrude

thought about another childhood memory.
She had always loved the excitement of
watching the freight trains speed past her
house. But what fascinated her the most
was the caboose at the end of each train.
Through the window of each caboose,
Gertrude could see a wooden table and a
small stove with a coffeepot. Sometimes
she could see men sitting at the table eat-
ing by the light of a lantern. Gertrude
always thought it would be fun to keep
house in a caboose.

She turned that memory into a story

about four children—Henry, Jessie, Violet, and Benny Alden—who lived in an old boxcar. The story was called *The Boxcar Children*.

Gertrude published the story in 1942. A few years later, she wrote *Surprise Island,* the second Boxcar book. In this story, the children solve a mystery, just as

The Boxcar Children

they do in the Boxcar books that followed. Gertrude wrote 19 Boxcar mysteries in all.

Gertrude's favorite place to write was her workroom at home.

It had an easy chair and wallpaper with her favorite flower— the violet. Gertrude wrote her stories by hand in blank books. First she wrote on the right-hand pages, then she turned the book upside down and wrote on the blank pages. She wrote most of her stories four times before they were just right.

The Boxcar Children books were some of the first mysteries for children. Gertrude loved thinking of new mysteries. She once said, "I would like to have done what they did. I'd still like to do it."

SAMANTHA
SAVES
THE WEDDING

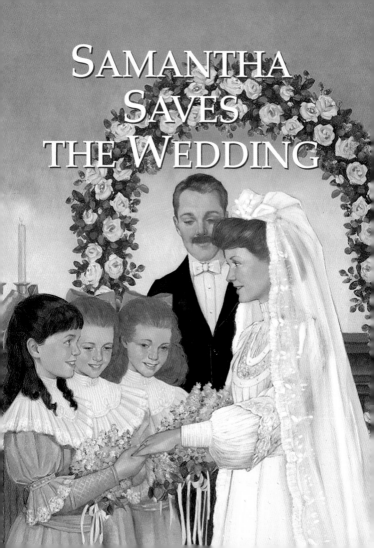

SAMANTHA SAVES THE WEDDING

R eady or not, here I come!" a voice
called out. Samantha Parkington
held her breath and tried not to move.
She didn't want to give away her hiding
place on the window seat behind the
curtain.

Suddenly the curtain was thrust
aside. A freckle-faced girl grinned at
Samantha.

"Oh, Agnes! You found me too
soon," said Samantha, laughing.

"I'm not Agnes," whispered the girl. "I'm Agatha. May I hide with you?"

"Sure," whispered Samantha. "Squinch in."

Agatha sat so close that her curls tickled Samantha's face and made her giggle. Soon both girls were giggling so much they didn't even hear Agnes enter the room.

The curtain was thrust aside again. "That was easy!" exclaimed Agnes. "You made more noise than the monkeys at the zoo."

Agnes looked exactly like Agatha. The twin girls were nine, just Samantha's age. Their older sister, Cornelia Pitt, was going to marry Samantha's Uncle Gard.

Samantha, Agnes, and Agatha were
going to be bridesmaids in the wedding.

Samantha and her grandmother had
been invited to stay at the Pitt family's
elegant town house in New York City for
the entire week before the wedding. They
had been with the Pitts for three days
so far, and Samantha thought it was the

most fun she had ever had.

Agnes kicked off her shoes and started jumping from bed to bed. "Come on!" she said. "Let's jump like monkeys."

"But Agnes," said Samantha. "You haven't found Alice yet." Alice was the twins' three-year-old sister.

"Oops! I forgot Alice," cried Agnes. "She always hides in the sewing room. Let's go."

All three girls rushed down the hall. Agnes and Agatha rushed everywhere. Uncle Gard said Agnes and Agatha were like woodpeckers: cheerful, redheaded, noisy, flighty, and into everything. The girls found Alice sitting on the

80

floor of the sewing room. A blanket covered most of her, but her feet stuck out. The older girls were too kind to laugh at Alice. Agnes lifted the blanket. "Here you are, Alice," she said. "I found you last of all."

Alice beamed. "That means I won," she said. "Let's play again."

"No, come jump on the beds with us," said Samantha. "We'll pretend we're monkeys."

"That won't take much pretending," said a deep voice. The girls turned to see Uncle Gard and Cornelia in the doorway. "Are you having fun with these rowdies, Sam?" he asked.

"Oh, yes!" said Samantha.

Cornelia gave Samantha a quick kiss. "We are all delighted to have you here," she said. "Now I need you and the twins to come with me. I've something to show you."

"Our bridesmaid dresses?" asked Agnes.

Cornelia smiled and nodded.

"Hurray!" shouted the twins.

"I want one, too," wailed Alice.

Samantha felt sorry for her. But then Uncle Gard said, "You come with me, Alice. We'll practice dancing. You *are* going to dance with me on my wedding day, aren't you?"

"Come on!" cried Agatha. The three girls ran down the stairs to Cornelia's

room and flung open the
door. When they saw
the lovely, lacy lavender
dresses lying on the bed,
they shrieked with delight.

Mrs. Pitt came into the room with
Grandmary. "Great Caesar's ghost,
girls!" she scolded. "Have a care for my
poor nerves!" Mrs. Pitt lowered herself
into a chair and held a handkerchief to
her forehead.

"Yes, ma'am," said the girls. They
couldn't wait to try on their new dresses
and were already halfway out of their
clothes.

Mrs. Pitt sighed and said to
Grandmary, "I think Agnes, Agatha, and

Samantha are too young to be bridesmaids, but Cornelia insisted upon it. I do hope they'll behave properly during the wedding."

Samantha was glad her face was hidden as she pulled her bridesmaid dress over her head. She was sure her cheeks were pink from hurt pride. How could Mrs. Pitt say such things? Samantha would *never* embarrass Cornelia—and especially not on her wedding day.

"I'm sure they'll behave like proper young ladies," replied Grandmary calmly.

"Young, indeed!" Mrs. Pitt said. "They are most exceptionally young."

"And they will be most exceptionally fine bridesmaids," said Cornelia. "I am sure."

Samantha poked her head out of her dress and flashed Cornelia a grateful smile.

When all the buttons were buttoned and sashes tied, Mrs. Pitt looked at the girls with a critical eye. "You look quite presentable," she said. "Take off the dresses now. Don't wrinkle them." And with that she swept out the door.

Grandmary paused long enough to say, "You young ladies look absolutely charming." And then she left, too.

"Cornelia," said Agatha when the girls had changed back into their usual clothes. "Please may we see your bridal gown?"

Cornelia opened the double doors of her wardrobe, and there it was—a creamy white dream of a dress decorated with tiny pearls from its high collar to its flowing train. "And here's the best part of all," said Cornelia. From behind the gown she carefully pulled a long white cascade of lace as light and fine as mist. "My veil."

"*Ooh,*" gasped the three girls.

Samantha sighed. "Oh, it's perfect."

Cornelia touched the veil gently. "Isn't it lovely?" she said. "I'll wear it only once, to mark the happiest day of my life."

It will be the happiest day of her life,
thought Samantha. *I'll make sure it is.*

"Cornelia," said Agnes. "When I
get married, may I wear this veil?"

"Yes, of course," said Cornelia.
"And you, too, Agatha. And you, too,
Samantha."

Samantha said softly, "Thank you.

But I . . . I already have a veil."

Everyone looked at Samantha with curiosity. "It was my mother's," she explained. "Grandmary said it belongs to me now. I've seen it only once or twice. It's in a box in the attic in Mount Bedford."

"How wonderful," said Cornelia. "Your mother has given you something precious to remember her by. I'm sure it's beautiful."

"Yes," said Samantha. "It's like your veil. It's long and white and puffy as a cloud."

Cornelia laughed. "My veil is as big as a cloud," she said. "In fact, I'd better find another place to keep it. I don't want it to be crushed." She grinned at the girls. "Well, my exceptional bridesmaids, run along now. I don't want you to use up all your good behavior before the wedding. Go find Alice and get into some mischief."

But the girls weren't interested in mischief. Instead, they decided to dress up as brides. Agatha found some old lace curtains in the sewing room. Each girl tied one around her waist to make a long, flowing skirt and draped another over her head to make a veil.

Suddenly Alice appeared. "I want a bride dress and veil, too!" she demanded. "Where's mine?"

"There are no more curtains," said

Agatha. "You can be the groom, Alice."

Alice frowned. "That's no fun!" she cried.

The girls had to admit she was right. So Samantha made a bride dress for Alice by pinning a pillowcase around her waist. For a veil, Alice wore one of Samantha's lace petticoats tied to her head with a ribbon.

The four girls practiced kneeling, sitting gracefully, and dancing. The older girls loved to swirl around and then sit down quickly to see their skirts and veils billow out around them. Alice was disappointed because her pillowcase and petticoat didn't swirl as well as the older girls' curtains did. So Samantha

promised her that the next time they
played dress-up she could have a better
skirt and veil. That satisfied Alice, and
the four brides played happily together
all afternoon.

The day of the wedding was wintry
gray and cold, but inside the
Pitts' house flowers bloomed
on every table. Delicious smells
floated out of the kitchen, the
doorbell rang constantly, and
excited voices filled the air. The four girls
spent the morning upstairs smearing
lemon paste on their faces to make their
freckles fade. They tied their hair up in

rags to make it curly. Samantha didn't actually have any freckles, and Agnes, Agatha, and Alice already had curly hair, but no one wanted to miss out on any of the fun.

About noon, the four girls wandered downstairs. When Mrs. Pitt saw their lemon-pasted faces, she cried, "Great Caesar's ghost, girls! Don't be in the way. The maid will come to help you dress at five. Until then, you older girls keep an eye on Alice." She fluttered her hands at them and said, "Shoo!"

"Yes, ma'am," said the girls. They scooted back upstairs.

Agatha asked restlessly, "What are

we supposed to do all afternoon?"

"Let's play hide-and-seek," said Samantha.

"No!" said Alice. "I want to play bride."

"We'll do that next," said Samantha. "Quick! Go hide now, Alice."

After a few minutes Samantha found Agnes and Agatha hiding under the beds. The three girls agreed that the lemon paste was making their faces itch, so they scrubbed it off. They pulled the rags out of their hair, too. They were just going to the sewing room to find Alice when Cornelia called to them.

"Come down, girls," she said. "Your bridesmaid bouquets are here!"

The older girls forgot all about Alice. They flew down the stairs. Grandmary, Mrs. Pitt, and Cornelia were waiting for them. Cornelia held three huge bouquets of lilacs in her arms.

"Here you are, ladies," she said. "Beautiful flowers for my beautiful bridesmaids."

The girls buried their faces in the bouquets to smell their lovely perfume.

Cornelia smiled and said, "Now take good care—" Suddenly the smile left her face and she gasped, "Alice!"

Everyone turned. Alice was coming downstairs draped in white from head to foot. Samantha stared, and then she

94

gasped, too. Alice was wearing Cornelia's wedding veil! She had hacked it in two and used one part for a skirt and the other part for a veil. The lace hung in tatters. Cornelia's veil was ruined— completely, utterly, totally ruined.

"Great Caesar's ghost!" exclaimed Mrs. Pitt.

"No," said Alice cheerfully. "I'm not a ghost. I'm a bride! Now I have a swirly skirt, too!"

For a moment, no one moved or said a word. Then Grandmary groaned. Mrs. Pitt collapsed into a chair. Agnes and Agatha wailed, "Oh, Alice!" Poor Alice burst into tears. She could tell she had done something terribly wrong.

Alice was wearing Cornelia's wedding veil!

Cornelia was very pale.

"You older girls go to your room," said Grandmary quietly.

The three girls trudged upstairs and flopped onto their beds. *If only we'd known Cornelia put her veil in the sewing room this morning!* thought Samantha. *We could have warned Alice not to touch it. But now . . .* "We've got to do something," she said in a determined voice.

"What can we do?" asked Agatha. "The veil is ruined. We can't fix it."

"And it's one o'clock. The wedding's in five hours," said Agnes. "There's not enough time to get a new veil."

"Not a new veil," said Samantha slowly. "An old veil. I have a plan."

Samantha found Uncle Gard in the study. He listened to her carefully. When she finished, he looked at his pocket watch and shook his head. "It's awfully risky, Sam," he said.

"I'm not sure there's enough time to get to Mount Bedford and back, especially in this icy weather. We don't want Cornelia to come down the aisle with no veil only to find she has no groom, either."

Samantha was impatient. "Please, Uncle Gard. We've got to try."

Uncle Gard stood up. "You're right, Sam. We *do* have to try. Let's go!"

Samantha held her coat over her head as she rushed out of the house

and climbed into Uncle Gard's automobile. Sleet slashed at the windshield.
Soon Samantha was being bounced and
bumped as the automobile lurched along
the icy, rutted roads. Uncle Gard was driv-
ing fast. Even so, it seemed to Samantha
that the trip was taking ages. The sleet
so blurred the view that she couldn't see
familiar landmarks along the way.

When they finally pulled up to
Grandmary's house, Samantha hardly
waited for the automobile to stop before
she jumped out and ran up the slippery
steps. She hammered on the door with
both fists and called out to the maid,
"Elsa! It's me! Hurry! Open the door!"

Elsa opened the door and exclaimed,

"Miss Samantha! Sakes alive! Whatever's going on?"

But Samantha did not stop. She ran past Elsa and pounded up the stairs to the attic. She pushed hatboxes, shoe boxes, and dusty boxes of books out of her way until she found it—the box holding her mother's veil.

Samantha lifted the lid and looked at the delicate veil. It smelled faintly of rose petals, a smell that always made her think of her mother. The soft smell of roses was reassuring. It was as if her mother were giving her blessing to the idea of letting Cornelia wear her veil. Samantha closed the box and carried it down the stairs and out to the automobile.

She and Uncle Gard did not talk much on the trip back to the city. Samantha knew it must be getting late because the sky was darkening. *Please let us get back in time,* she thought. *Please!*

At half past five, Samantha and Uncle Gard walked into the Pitts' town house—and into an uproar. "Where on earth have you two been?" cried Mrs. Pitt. She pushed her way toward them through a swarm of maids and musicians, waiters and florists.

Samantha left Uncle Gard to explain. She hurried up the stairs to Cornelia's room and tapped on the door.

"Why, Samantha!" said Cornelia when she opened the door. She was already wearing her wedding gown. "Everyone's been worried. Where have you been?"

"I have something for you, Cornelia," said Samantha. She set the box on the floor, knelt by it, and opened the lid. "It's my mother's veil," she said.

Cornelia sank to her knees next to Samantha. Slowly, she lifted the veil out of the box. "Oh," she said with a sigh. "It's so beautiful! I am honored to wear it." Cornelia had tears in her eyes, but she laughed as she said, "Oh, thank you, Samantha, thank you!"

Candles glowed in every window. The music began. Exactly on cue, Agnes, then Agatha, and then Samantha walked down the flower-lined aisle to the graceful arch of greenery in front of the Pitts' hearth. Mrs. Pitt, Alice, and Grandmary smiled at the girls from the first row of chairs.

Uncle Gard stood by the hearth next to the minister. His tie looked as if he had tied it in a hurry. His hair was still damp. But he looked happy. His smile broadened as the three girls walked toward him. He winked at Samantha.

Everyone murmured in delight as they watched Cornelia walking slowly

*Samantha and Agnes and Agatha stood shoulder to shoulder—
three most exceptionally happy bridesmaids.*

down the aisle on her father's arm. Through the fine lace of the veil, Cornelia smiled at Uncle Gard. Then she, too, winked at Samantha.

Samantha felt her heart fill with love. She and Agnes and Agatha stood shoulder to shoulder—three most exceptionally happy bridesmaids.

LOOKING BACK

WEDDINGS IN 1904

A courting couple

When Samantha was growing up, weddings were as elaborate and as elegant as a couple could afford. Society weddings like Uncle Gard and Cornelia's were splendid affairs that were filled with tradition and followed the rules of proper behavior.

Young ladies and gentlemen of

society met when they were formally introduced at dinner parties, dances, or balls. They might also meet when a young lady's mother invited gentlemen to *call on*, or visit, her daughter.

Once a couple had been introduced, they were permitted to *court*, or spend time together. They might sit in the young lady's parlor talking or playing games. Or they could go bicycling or roller-skating, on sleigh rides, or to amusement parks.

A gentleman handing a rose to his sweetheart

When a gentleman was ready to propose, he asked his young lady for her hand in marriage. If she accepted, he asked her parents for their approval. Once they agreed, he slipped a ring onto the third finger of her left hand. This tradition followed the belief that a vein ran from that finger directly to the heart.

During the engagement, couples exchanged love tokens, such as flowers, locks of hair, or small portraits. They also sent each other love letters and even used their postage stamps to communicate. If the stamp was placed upside down on the left-hand corner of the envelope, it meant "I love you." If it was on the line with the recipient's name, it meant "Accept my love."

Once a young lady was engaged, she had to plan her wedding. The first thing she did was decide on a date. For many brides-to-be, the day, the month, even the hour

Some young ladies kept their love letters in silk pockets.

of the wedding had important meaning. Each day of the week and month of the year had a rhyme that told its importance. June was one of the most popular months because it might mean an exciting honey-moon: "Marry when June roses grow, over land and sea you'll go." Some people believed that the best day of all to marry was on the groom's birthday.

Many brides spent months planning their weddings. They read ladies' magazines and newspaper accounts of society weddings, such as Consuelo Vanderbilt's wedding to the Duke of Marlborough—the most fashionable wedding of the time.

The most important thing a bride had to plan was her bridal outfit. Turn-of-the-century brides wore white silk or satin wedding gowns with graceful, sweeping trains.

Consuelo Vanderbilt and the Duke of Marlborough

The dresses were often embroidered with delicate flowers, pearls, lace, and ribbons.

When they planned their bridal outfits, many brides followed the saying:

Something old,
Something new,
Something borrowed,
Something blue,
And a silver sixpence in her shoe.

In 1906, the newspapers wrote about White House bride Alice Roosevelt, the daughter of President Theodore Roosevelt. She wore a cream satin dress with an 18-foot silver brocade train. Soon after the wedding, ladies' magazines reported that silver bridal trimmings were the newest fashion.

Alice Roosevelt

Brides often carried large bouquets. In the Victorian language of flowers, each flower a bride carried had a special meaning. Roses meant love, lilacs meant first love, lilies of the valley meant the couple would receive much happiness, and orange blossoms meant they would have many children. Bridesmaids carried *tussie-mussies,* or small bouquets of flowers. Many brides chose their sisters or

Bridal bouquet

their closest friends to be their bridesmaids. Some weddings had as many as eight or ten bridesmaids.

Before the wedding, the bride and
her bridesmaids celebrated with a lunch-
eon and a special "bridesmaids' cake."
It had charms baked inside. Each bridesmaid could tell her future from the charm
she found in her piece of cake. An
anchor meant adventure, a horse-
shoe meant good luck, a heart
meant true love, a flower meant
blossoming love, a key meant a
happy home, and a ring meant
a blissful marriage.

A bride and groom got married
at church or at the home of the bride's
parents. Wherever the ceremony, the decorations were as elaborate as the couple's
family could afford. Evergreens, potted

palms, and huge sprays of flowers decorated the church. At home, rooms were decorated with hearts or bells made from flowers. Many couples said their vows under a flower-covered

A wedding under a trellis and bell

trellis with a good-luck symbol such as a bell or a dove hanging from the arch. After the ceremony, there might be food, entertainment, and dancing.

As the couple left for their honeymoon, the wedding party might throw slippers at their carriage. If a slipper landed on top of the carriage, the couple was promised good luck forever.

SAMANTHA'S
BLUE BICYCLE

SAMANTHA'S
BLUE BICYCLE

Grandmary!" Samantha called out
excitedly. "It's Uncle Gard and Aunt
Cornelia! They're here!"

Down the stairs Samantha flew, and
out the big doors to the front porch. She
took the steps in a single leap and threw
herself into Gard's arms just as he climbed
out of his auto. "Oh, Uncle Gard!" she
said. "We missed you so!"

"We missed you too, Sam," said Gard
as he hugged her. "We're glad to be back."

This was Gard and Cornelia's first visit to Mount Bedford since their wedding. After their honeymoon they had taken a few days to settle into their new town house in New York City. Samantha had been waiting impatiently for this visit. She wanted it to be perfect, so Gard and Cornelia would come visit often. She did not want to be left out of their lives now that they were married.

Grandmary came down the steps and hugged Cornelia hello. Then she tilted her cheek to receive Gard's kiss. "Gardner, dear," she said. "It has been entirely too dull and quiet here without you and your dreadful automobile."

Cornelia smiled at Samantha. "What a pretty pinafore!" she said. "Is it new?"

"Yes," said Samantha happily. She held out the skirt of the ruffly white pinafore. "It's special for your visit."

"It makes you look very tall," said Cornelia. "I believe you've grown a foot since we've been away."

Gard stared at Samantha's feet. "Still only two that I can see," he joked. "Thank goodness! Otherwise she'd have a hard time using the present we brought her." With a dramatic *whoosh,* Gard pulled the canvas tarp off the back of the auto. Samantha gasped when she saw what was there: three shiny new bicycles.

"We got them in England," said Gard

as he lifted the bicycles down. "They're the very latest models."

"I told Gard it was high time you had a bicycle, Samantha," said Cornelia. "I loved cycling when I was your age. It's so fast and free! I'm sure you'll love it, too."

"And here's the best part of all," added Gard. "We're going to leave the bicycles here in Mount Bedford. Just think of the fun we'll have, the three of us, bicycling together!"

The three of us . . . Samantha was so happy she couldn't speak.

"This one is yours, Sam," said Gard. He rolled a beautiful blue bicycle toward her.

"Oh, thank you," said Samantha. She

put one hand on the shiny handlebars and the other on the leather seat and looked up at her grandmother. "Please, Grandmary," she asked eagerly, "may I keep it?" She was worried, for she knew very well that Grandmary thought bicycles were dangerous and not quite proper for young ladies. That's why Samantha had never had one, even though she was nine years old.

Grandmary sighed. "In my day," she said, "bicycles were ridden in circus acts by women wearing tights. Soon everywhere you looked there were women riding bicycles on the streets. Some of them wore hideous, short, puffy trousers called bloomers. We referred to those women as Bloomer

Girls." She sniffed. "Most unladylike!"

Cornelia spoke up gently. "A lady is a lady no matter what she's wearing," she said. "I hardly think Samantha will act improperly on her bicycle."

"Indeed not!" Grandmary replied tartly. She turned and smiled at Samantha. "I can see that you have your heart set on riding this bicycle with Gard and Cornelia, dear girl," she said. "You may keep it if you promise to be careful."

"I will," promised Samantha.

"Well then, hop on, Sam!" said Gard. He held the bike. When Samantha sat on the seat, the skirt of her dress and her pinafore and her petticoats billowed around her. She tucked them all under

her legs to get them out of the way. Then
Gard pushed and she pedaled and the
wheels turned, and there she was, riding
the bicycle with Gard running alongside,
holding her steady!

"Hurray!" Cornelia cheered.

The ruffles on Samantha's pinafore
fluttered, and her heart did, too. Riding
the bicycle was harder than she had
thought it would be. She tried to keep
the front tire from wobbling, and she tried
to keep a smile on her face, but she was
nervous. She was afraid she would topple
over if it were not for Gard's firm hold.

"Are you ready for me to let go?"
Gard asked after a few minutes.

Samantha gulped. "Yes," she said,

*There she was, riding the bicycle with Gard
running alongside, holding her steady!*

wanting to impress Gard and Cornelia by being a quick learner. Gard let go, and she rode the bike in a big, slow, shaky circle on the driveway.

When she stopped, Gard and Cornelia clapped and cheered. "I knew you'd get the hang of it right away!" Cornelia praised her.

"Let's go to the park," Gard suggested with enthusiasm. "There are lots of paths there, so you won't have to go round in circles."

"Dear me!" said Grandmary. "Don't you think it's a bit too soon?"

"I think it's up to Sam," said Gard. "If she's plucky enough to try the park, then we should let her. What do you say, Sam?"

Samantha was *not* sure she wanted to go to the park, but she *was* sure she wanted to be plucky. "Let's go," she said.

"That's my girl!" said Gard proudly.

❧

The park was crowded with bicyclists enjoying the sunny spring day. Samantha thought they were all cycling rather fast, as if their bicycles were being hurried along by the brisk spring breeze.

"Be careful," Grandmary cautioned from her perch on a park bench. "Don't go too fast."

"You go first, Sam," said Gard as they wheeled their bicycles to the path that ran alongside the lake. "Cornelia and I will follow and keep an eye on you."

"All right," said Samantha. Feeling awkward and unsteady, she mounted her bicycle. She wanted to tuck her skirts out of the way, but there wasn't time. Her bicycle started rolling forward before she had even pushed down on the pedals!

The path was wide, but it wasn't as flat or as smooth as the driveway. It dropped off sharply on her right along the bank of the lake. Samantha pedaled slowly, concentrating as hard as she could on not falling.

Suddenly she felt a tug. She looked down. Her skirt had caught in the bike chain! She started to yank it free, but just then Uncle Gard shouted, "Watch out!"

Samantha looked up. To her horror, she saw that a cyclist was flying straight toward her at top speed! In a panic, Samantha swerved hard to the right. Her bike lurched off the path and bounced down the bank, out of control.

"Help!" she shrieked. She struggled to steer, but the front wheel wobbled violently. *Crash!* The bicycle smashed into a huge rock. In a terrible tangle, Samantha and the bicycle fell right into the mucky water at the edge of the lake. *Splash!*

"Samantha!" shouted Gard and Cornelia as they rushed down the slope to help her. "Are you all right?"

Samantha bit her lip and nodded,

*Samantha looked up. To her horror, she saw that
a cyclist was flying straight toward her at top speed!*

though she was fighting back tears. Her ankle was twisted, her stockings torn, and she had a bad scrape on one hand. Her new pinafore was mud-spattered, grass-stained, and grease-streaked. Her skirt was so badly twisted around the chain that she had to rip it to get it free.

Grandmary appeared at the top of the bank. "Merciful heavens!" she exclaimed. "It's a wonder you weren't killed! I hope no bones are broken."

"No, Mother," Gard called up to her as he helped Samantha stand. "Sam's fine."

"The poor child's had enough fool-ishness for one day," said Grandmary firmly. "We're going home—right now."

When Grandmary said *poor child,*

Cornelia got a stubborn look in her eye. "Samantha," she asked, "do you want to go home now?"

With all her heart, Samantha wanted to go home. She hated the idea of getting back on the bicycle. But she hated the idea of disappointing Gard and Cornelia even more. She wiped her hands on her ruined pinafore and tried to think what to say.

"Got to get back on the horse that threw you, right, Sam?" said Uncle Gard.

Samantha looked at the muddy bicycle and noticed something. With tremendous relief she said, "I don't think I *can* get back on, Uncle Gard. The front tire is flat."

Gard picked up

the bicycle and looked at the tire. "You're right," he said. "We'll have to have it fixed. No more riding today."

"What a shame!" said Cornelia with a sigh.

"Don't be too disappointed, Sam," Gard said as they walked back to the automobile. "We'll try again soon. Meanwhile, you'll have time to practice."

Practice? thought Samantha. *I never want to get on that bicycle again as long as I live!*

One afternoon a few days later, when Samantha came home from school, Grandmary said, "Hawkins has fixed your bicycle."

"That's nice," said Samantha dully.

"He will help you if you feel you must practice," Grandmary added.

"*No!*" said Samantha. "I mean, no thank you, not today. I can't! I . . . I have too much schoolwork to do."

"Very well," said Grandmary.

Samantha could tell by the look on Grandmary's face that she was a little surprised. Samantha wished she could tell Grandmary how fearful she was of the bicycle, but she was too ashamed of her fear to tell the truth.

For the next week, whenever Samantha walked past the carriage house, she looked away, thinking about the bicycle sitting inside unused. Whenever she remembered her scary fall, she shivered. She wished she *had* broken some bones. She wished she had damaged the bicycle beyond all repair. She wished she'd get the chicken pox again, or that winter would come back and cover everything with snow. Anything, *anything* to excuse her from riding that hateful bicycle.

Then, on Saturday afternoon, the telephone rang.

"Hello!" said Gard's cheery voice. "Guess what? Cornelia and I are coming out to Mount Bedford next weekend, and we're bringing Cornelia's sisters with us. Agnes and Agatha are crackerjack cyclists. We'll all go on a long bicycle ride together and bring a picnic. Doesn't that sound like fun, Sam?"

"Mmm-hmm," said Samantha, her heart sinking.

"Keep practicing," said Gard. "See you soon! Good-bye!"

"Good-bye," said Samantha. After she hung up the telephone, she stood next to it for a moment, deep in misery. She pictured herself standing with Grandmary on the front porch, waving good-bye to Gard, Cornelia, Agnes, and Agatha as they tootled off merrily on their bicycles, leaving her behind. How could she tell Gard and Cornelia that she hated the bicycle they'd given her and that they'd *never* ride together again?

In desperation, Samantha went to the carriage house. She wheeled her bicycle out onto the driveway and climbed on nervously. She took a deep breath, pushed down on one pedal, and rolled forward. Just as before, the front tire wobbled  wildly, her skirt got caught in the chain, and *crash!* Down she fell on the driveway.

"I can't do it! I can't!" she wailed to no one. She pulled her skirt free, kicked the bike away from her in anger, then bent her head and cried in shame and frustration.

Grandmary came out of the house. She knelt next to Samantha and put her arms around her. She let Samantha finish crying before she asked, "Are you all right, dear?"

"I hate that bicycle!" Samantha said fiercely. "I'm scared to ride it. Every time I do, my skirt gets tangled, I lose control, and I fall. Uncle Gard said I was plucky, but I'm not. I'm afraid."

"And yet you tried again just now," said Grandmary. "I saw you."

Samantha tried to explain. "Riding bicycles was something Uncle Gard and Aunt Cornelia and I were going to do *together*," she said slowly. "If I can't ride, I'm afraid they won't visit very often . . ."

"And we'll be left out of their lives," Grandmary finished for her.

Samantha nodded.

"Well," said Grandmary, "perhaps I can help you."

Samantha was surprised. "But I thought you didn't approve of the bicycle," she said. "I thought you didn't want me to ride it."

Grandmary smiled. "I would not have chosen a bicycle for you myself," she said. "But I don't want you to be left out of the fun. Besides, it's you who'll have to ride the bicycle, not I. Do you think you can do it?"

Samantha took a deep breath. She looked at the bicycle, then she looked at Grandmary. "I really want to try," she said.

"Very well," said Grandmary. "Here's what we'll do . . ."

இ

Saturday was bright and beautiful.

"It's just the day for a bike ride!" exclaimed Gard as he helped Cornelia, Agnes, and Agatha out of the auto at Grandmary's house.

"Indeed it is," said Grandmary, coming down the steps to greet them.

Samantha opened her window and called, "Hello, everyone!"

"Hello, Sam!" Uncle Gard called back. "Are you ready for some fun?"

"I sure am!" answered Samantha. "I'll be right there!" When Samantha burst out of the front doors, all of the visitors gasped.

"Jiminy!" exclaimed Agnes. "Bloomers!"

"Bloomers!" Agatha sighed enviously. "Samantha, you're so lucky! I can't believe Grandmary lets you wear them."

"They were Grandmary's idea!" said Samantha. "Now I don't have to worry

about my skirt getting caught. I've been wearing bloomers all week while I've practiced riding. Watch this!"

Samantha hopped on her bicycle and rode in a big circle around the driveway without wobbling a bit.

"Why, Grandmary," said Cornelia. "You astonish me."

Grandmary's eyes twinkled. "A lady is a lady no matter what she's wearing," she said. Then she and Cornelia laughed together.

"Come on, everyone," called Samantha. "Let's go!" Samantha led the way on her beautiful blue bicycle. At the end of the driveway, she turned and waved good-bye to Grandmary. Then she rode off down the road.

"Hey, Sam!" Uncle Gard called after her. "Wait for us!"

LOOKING BACK

BICYCLING IN 1904

When Samantha was growing up in the early 1900s, bicycling was a popular pastime for everyone, including women and girls. But it had taken bicycle inventors many tries before they discovered a design that was easy and safe for women and girls to ride.

Some of the earliest bicycles had big wooden wheels with iron tires. These bicycles were called *boneshakers* because they were such a bumpy ride! Later, in the 1880s, bicycles with huge front wheels were

A boneshaker

designed. The "high-wheeler" became so popular that people began to call it the *ordinary*. But riding the ordinary took skill and balance, and wearing a skirt made it almost impossible.

By the early 1890s, the *safety bike* had been invented. It was the first bike that women and girls could ride easily. The bike had enclosed gears that kept skirts from getting tangled in the chains. The safety bike also had two equal-sized

A safety bike

wheels and a dropped frame with no crossbar. In 1898, the coaster brake was added to the safety bike. To use this brake, the rider pushed the pedal back to make the bicycle stop. All of these features made riding the safety bike a breeze!

To make riding even easier, many women and girls also changed their style of clothing. They started wearing *bloomers,* or full pants gathered at the knee.

A "Bloomer Girl"

When people first saw women in bloomers, they were flabbergasted. Many people did not think that bloomers were appropriate clothing for women. But women and girls continued to wear them. By 1895, "Bloomer Girls" were a common sight in American cities.

Soon people accepted this change, and clothes that fit more active lifestyles became fashionable. Women began wearing shorter skirts and split skirts. Cycling skirts were often brown or tan—a proper young lady wouldn't want the dust and dirt to show! Tight-fitting corsets made it difficult for women to breathe

A split skirt

A health corset

while bicycling, so the *health corset* or *bicycle waist* became popular. This corset had a straight front, so it did not press on a woman's abdomen when she was riding.

In the 1890s, a bicycling craze swept America. Everyone was cycling, and towns formed cycling clubs. The Metropolitan Academy in New York City set aside an area for women to learn to bicycle. In the winter, men and women attended "musical rides," where they pedaled in circles to the music of a live orchestra.

Indoor bicycling clubs allowed people to ride their bicycles year-round.

Another popular New York City club was the *Michaux* (mee-show) Club. It was named after Pierre Michaux, a Frenchman who manufactured one of the first two-wheeled bicycles. The Michaux Club began in 1895 as a place for people to ride in the winter. Men and women had separate riding sessions. In the morning, women received their riding lessons. After lunch, they rode to music and enjoyed tea served in the clubrooms. Women also took part in "ten-pin rides,"

where they demonstrated their skills by riding their bicycles in and out of a line of bowling pins.

Riders also showed off their skills in *gymkhana* (jim-KAH-nuh) festivals—a new craze from India. The bicyclists wore elaborate red and white uniforms and rode bicycles decorated with red and white ribbons. The festival was full of activities to do on bicycles, such as relay races, fancy-riding exhibitions, and a grand march. At the end of the evening, men and women "danced" the Virginia Reel on their bicycles.

These European ads show how popular gymkhana festivals were overseas, too.

Many couples thought the bicycle was romantic. They went for bicycle rides together or rode *tandem* bicycles, which were built for two riders. One young woman even rode off on the family tandem to elope with her young gentleman!

For many women, the bicycle was a "freedom machine." Before bicycles, people used horses to get around. Girls weren't usually allowed to drive or ride horses by themselves. But bicycles easily took a girl almost anywhere she wanted to go.

A tandem wedding

Not everyone thought this new freedom machine was a good thing. The writer
of this poem certainly didn't!

Before she got her bicycle,
She sometimes used to make
The beds and wash the dishes,
And help her mother bake.
But now she's got her bicycle,
She doesn't do a thing
About the house, but day and night
She's always on the wing!

SAMANTHA'S
SPECIAL TALENT

SAMANTHA'S
SPECIAL TALENT

Rain pounded the roof of the old Mount Bedford Public Library as Samantha and her friend Ida read together at a small corner table. Samantha was caught up in the adventures of an Amazon River explorer. The fearless explorer was just about to be attacked by crocodiles when—*plop!*—a drop of water landed on Samantha's head.

Samantha looked up. *Plop!* Another drop hit her eye. Water was dripping through the ceiling of the old library.

Samantha slid her book to Ida's side of the table and hurried over to the librarian, a tall, red-bearded man who was sitting at the circulation desk. Above his desk, a poster announced:

BUILD A BETTER LIBRARY!
MEETING AT 4 P.M. SATURDAY, MAY 5TH
THE MOUNT BEDFORD OPERA HOUSE

"It's leaking over there, Mr. Hardy," said Samantha, pointing to the ceiling. "I hope the library can be fixed soon."

The librarian nodded. "We're trying to raise the money, Samantha. But not many people come to our meetings. Sometimes I wonder how we'll ever get support." He sighed.

"I wish I could help," Samantha offered.

Mr. Hardy reached under his desk. He pulled out a battered tin bucket. "How about putting a bucket under that leak?"

As Samantha carried the bucket to her table, she wondered, *Why won't people come to the library meetings? Everybody always comes to our school meetings.* Suddenly an idea hit her. She hurried back to the librarian. "Mr. Hardy," she burst out, "maybe we could have a talent show!"

Mr. Hardy looked up. "Pardon?"

"We have a talent show at school every year, and all the families come," Samantha explained excitedly. "Maybe if we had a talent show at the Opera House, people would come to the library meeting."

163

"It's an interesting idea," Mr. Hardy said slowly. "But Saturday is only four days away. Could a talent show be organized so quickly?"

"I'm sure it could," Samantha said. "I bet lots of children would like to perform. I know *I'd* like to be in a show."

Mr. Hardy stroked his red beard. Finally he said, "I'm giving a talk to the Ladies' Club this afternoon. They might assist with a show like that. After all, any money you raise would be a help, even if—" *Plop! Plop!*

A second leak had opened in the ceiling above Mr. Hardy's desk. He grabbed another bucket to catch the rain. *Spang* went the water as it hit the tin. Mr. Hardy laughed. "Even if it's only a drop in the bucket!"

164

Samantha rushed to her table. "Ida, listen!" she exclaimed, and she told her friend about the proposed talent show.

Ida put down her mystery. "Jeepers, Samantha, it's a wonderful idea! I'll help make tickets."

"I thought maybe you and I could perform together," Samantha suggested. "We could dance or sing a duet or—"

"No! I could never go onstage!" Ida interrupted, shaking her head so hard that her hair swung across her face. "Besides, aren't you going to play the piano, like you always do?"

"I don't want to play the piano again," Samantha said, looking down at the scarred wooden table. "Edith Eddleton always plays the piano, and she's ten times better than I am." Samantha paused. "But if we did something together . . ."

"I'm sorry, Samantha, but I'd die of fright if I had to go onstage," Ida said firmly. Suddenly thunder exploded outside. Both girls jumped. "It would be even scarier than *that*," Ida added.

The two girls giggled. Then Samantha said, "Ida, you're the best artist in the class. Would you draw posters for the show?"

"That would be easy!" Ida said. "I hope the Ladies' Club says yes to the idea."

"I hope so, too," Samantha agreed. *And*, she thought, *I hope I can think of an act to do!*

❧

At school the next day, excitement spread when the teacher, Miss Stevens, announced there would be a children's talent show at the Opera House on Saturday afternoon.

"Samantha is helping to organize this event," Miss Stevens said. "If you would like to perform, talk to her during recess." The whole class turned to look at Samantha, who tried to smile confidently.

"The show will aid the library, so I hope you'll participate," Miss Stevens added.

Clarisse Van Sicklen, the class know-it-all, raised her hand. "How can one talent show pay for a library?" she asked skeptically.

Miss Stevens peered over her glasses. "Big projects may have small beginnings, Clarisse."

Another girl raised her hand. Samantha was surprised to see that it was Marguerite DuBois, the new student from France. Marguerite's widowed mother, Madame DuBois, taught French at Lessing's Boys School. Marguerite rarely spoke in class. When she did talk, some girls snickered at her accent.

"Mees Stevens, what ees a 'talent show'?" the French girl asked shyly.

"It's a show where girls and boys perform their special talents, such as singing or dancing," Miss Stevens explained.

"Doesn't Marguerite know anything?" Clarisse whispered, loud enough for the other girls to hear. Marguerite blushed bright red.

Miss Stevens had turned to the black-board. "Let's return to mathematics, girls. You may discuss the talent show at recess."

When the recess bell clanged, Helen Whitney hurried to Samantha's desk. "My two sisters and I sing together," she announced.

"Wonderful!" Samantha said. She pulled out a crisp sheet of new paper. "The Whitney Sisters—singing," she wrote carefully. She had her first act for the talent show!

Clarisse and Edith Eddleton marched over together. "I'll play my best piano sonata," Edith announced. "I should be first on the program since I always win the school talent show."

Samantha rolled her eyes. Edith always insisted she should be first. "I'll do my best," Samantha promised.

"Put me down for the violin," Clarisse proclaimed.

More girls clustered around Samantha's desk. Ruth Adams and Elisabeth Turner offered to perform a clarinet duo. Emmeline Andrews revealed that she could do a dramatic reading of "The Song of Hiawatha." Everyone was talking excitedly when Samantha noticed Marguerite sitting alone at her desk.

"Marguerite, would you like to be in the show?" Samantha asked.

"Her?" Clarisse sneered. "She doesn't even know what a talent show is!"

The French girl blushed again. Samantha's own face grew hot. "Don't pay attention, Marguerite," Samantha said. "Clarisse just wishes she could speak French as well as you do."

Clarisse tossed her head. "Come on, let's go outside," she urged Edith and the others. They filed out, leaving Samantha

171

and Marguerite alone in the classroom.

Samantha walked over to Marguerite. "Would you like to dance in the show? Miss Stevens said you took ballet lessons in Paris."

"To go onstage alone—it is difficult, yes?" Marguerite asked.

"Yes—I mean no!" Samantha exclaimed. "It's fun, and it's for a good cause."

"I would need music," Marguerite said. "At home, my mother plays the violin when I dance. Yet she gives lessons on Saturdays. I do not know if she could play at a show."

"If your mother can't come, I'll play the piano for you," Samantha volunteered.

Marguerite's face brightened. "*Merci,*

Samantha! Are you sure?"

"I'm sure." Samantha added to her list "Marguerite—ballet."

After school, several neighborhood boys signed up for the show. Ida's brother, Winston, said that he would do his "famous magic act." Fred Whitney insisted that his talking parrot, Pete, should perform. Henry Van Sicklen bragged that he played trumpet "better than any kid in Mount Bedford." Even Samantha's bratty neighbor, Eddie Ryland, wanted to be included in the show.

"I can juggle better than anyone," Eddie declared. "I'm bound to win first prize."

By the end of the day, Samantha had ten acts scheduled. As she and Grandmary sat in the parlor that evening, she proudly displayed her list of performers.

"You've worked very hard," Grandmary said. "But I don't see your name on this list."

"If Madame DuBois can't come to the show, I'll play for Marguerite," Samantha replied. She looked down. "I can't think of any act to do on my own. I don't have any special talents."

"You're a very talented young lady," Grandmary said gently. "Have faith in your abilities."

Samantha thought about what Grandmary had said. Before bedtime, she wrote a list of her talents to see if one might be useful in the show:

My Talents
Singing—I'm good, but Helen
and her sisters are better!
Piano—I'm quite good, but
Edith is much better.
Boating—I'm good, but there's
no lake at the Opera House!
Swimming—See above.
Reading—I'm very good, but
I don't like reading aloud.

What should I do? Samantha wondered.
I have to think of something by Saturday!

But during the next two days, Samantha
was so busy organizing the show, she had
no time to plan an act. After school Thurs-
day, she and Ida made posters and put them
up around town. Samantha noticed that her
posters looked plain compared with Ida's,
which had fancy lettering and borders.

"How do you make yours so pretty?"

"I've always liked drawing," Ida said with a shrug. "It's just a talent, I suppose."

I wish I knew what my talent was, Samantha thought.

After school Friday, Samantha and Ida invited Marguerite to help make tickets. "*Oui!*" she agreed, her eyes glistening with happiness.

The three girls sat under a tree in Ida's yard with ginger cookies and glasses of milk. While they folded and cut, Samantha asked Marguerite if her mother could play in the show.

"She will come if she must," said Marguerite as she maneuvered her scissors through the paper.

176

"I've always liked drawing," Ida said with a shrug.
"It's just a talent, I suppose."

"She has lessons to teach, though, so it would be difficult. Perhaps we should practice with the piano at the rehearsal tonight. Do you know *Swan Lake*?"

"No, but it won't be a problem," Samantha said confidently. *I'm not as good as Edith, but I can play the piano,* she thought.

The three girls worked and chatted until Samantha looked up and saw the sun glowing red on the horizon. "Oh, no!" she said. "We'll be late to rehearsal!"

Ida stayed behind to arrange the tickets while Samantha and Marguerite brushed grass off their dresses and hurried to the Opera House. The Ladies' Club had asked Miss Stevens, who produced the school shows, to direct the rehearsal. The teacher was watching each act with a critical eye.

"Louder, girls!" she told the Whitney sisters. "Sing so everyone will hear you!"

Miss Stevens advised Fred to put a leash on his parrot. "Your parrot may become nervous when it performs," she cautioned.

Glancing around the big Opera House, Samantha realized she might become nervous, too. Marguerite's dance was the last act of the show, and as the girls waited to rehearse, Samantha studied the music. It looked harder than she had expected. *I wish I'd had time to practice,* she thought.

When Miss Stevens finally called them up, Marguerite jumped gracefully onto the wooden stage. Samantha wiped her sweating palms and sat at the big piano.

She quickly discovered that *Swan Lake* was even harder than it looked. As she struggled to find the notes, she kept losing the tempo. *Marguerite may be a swan,* Samantha thought, *but I feel like a turtle.*

"Faster, Samantha," Miss Stevens urged.

Samantha tried, but it was no use. The more she and Marguerite worked to keep pace with each other, the more they both seemed out of step.

Most of the other performers had gone home, but Eddie Ryland had stayed to practice juggling. Now he sneered at the girls. "You call that dancing? My dog dances better!"

"Go home, Eddie," said Miss Stevens.

As soon as Eddie left, Samantha

Eddie sneered at the girls.
"You call that dancing? My dog dances better!"

stopped playing. "We need your mother," she told Marguerite glumly. The other girl nodded.

"It ees not easy, Samantha," Marguerite said comfortingly. "Thank you for trying."

Samantha felt like crying. *I'm not good at anything,* she thought. But she tried to act cheerful. "It's probably just as well I won't be playing the piano tomorrow," she said. "Ida and I will be busy selling tickets."

Saturday turned out to be even more hectic than Samantha had imagined. So many friends and family members lined up for the show that Samantha and Ida sold more than a hundred tickets.

"Jiminy!" Samantha exclaimed when she saw all the money they had collected. "That should help the library fund. Let's go see the show!"

Grandmary had saved the girls two front-row seats. They slid into them just in time for Edith's piano sonata. Samantha felt a stab of jealousy as she listened to Edith's nearly perfect performance. *Everyone is more talented than I am,* she thought.

Not all the acts went perfectly, however. Emmeline forgot a verse of "Hiawatha," Clarisse's violin squeaked, and the Whitney sisters sang so softly, they could barely be heard. Fred's big green parrot tried to fly away, but luckily Fred had put him on a leash.

Winston's magic show went smoothly until he reached dramatically into his black hat to pull out a rabbit. The rabbit, however, popped out from under the table and scampered across the stage. The audience clapped and laughed.

The next act was Eddie Ryland's juggling. Samantha was impressed by his skill. He managed three balls and made it look easy.

The last act was Marguerite's ballet solo. Marguerite entered the stage wearing a full white skirt that looked like a real ballerina's, but she seemed pale and nervous.

Samantha crossed her fingers. *I encouraged her to do this,* she thought. *I hope it goes well.*

As Madame DuBois played the opening notes, Marguerite took a deep breath and began to dance. At first she seemed unsure of herself. But as the music continued, she moved with greater confidence. Finally, like a bird that has just learned to fly, Marguerite soared across the stage, her shimmering skirt swirling with every turn and leap.

When she took her bow, the audience applauded enthusiastically. Samantha and Ida exchanged happy smiles.

As the judges put their heads together, Samantha squirmed in her seat. She wanted so much for Marguerite to do well! Finally, the judges gave their results to Mr. Hardy.

The librarian cleared his throat. "As I announce the winners, please come onstage. Third prize . . . Edward Ryland." Eddie swaggered up to receive a handsome bronze medal. Samantha sighed. It was a shame anyone as mean as Eddie should win anything.

Mr. Hardy continued, "Second prize . . . Marguerite DuBois." Samantha clapped so hard, she almost fell off her seat. *I bet Clarisse won't make fun of Marguerite now!* she thought.

Marguerite shyly accepted a beautiful silver medal, while Madame DuBois beamed.

Mr. Hardy held up a fancy gold medal. "For first prize . . . Edith Eddleton!"

Samantha applauded. Edith was annoying, but she did play the piano beautifully.

After the applause faded, Mr. Hardy held up his hand. "Before we talk about the library, I'd like Samantha Parkington to come up."

Samantha looked about in surprise. *He can't mean me,* she thought. *I wasn't even in the show.* Grandmary, however, nudged her gently. Reluctantly, she climbed onto the stage.

"Today's talent show was Samantha's idea, and she helped organize it," Mr. Hardy announced. "I'm grateful for the money raised, and I'm impressed by Samantha's talents as a leader."

Samantha felt her face flush. Looking

*"Today's talent show was Samantha's idea,
and she helped organize it," Mr. Hardy announced.*

at the audience, she saw Grandmary watching her with fond, proud eyes. *I guess Grandmary was right—I do have a special talent,* she thought. The audience clapped loudly.

Mr. Hardy smiled. "I'm all out of medals, Samantha. But if you come to the library on Monday, you can be the first person to get a card for the new library we're going to build."

"That would be wonderful," Samantha said with a grin. "Reading is one of my best talents!"

189

LOOKING BACK

GREAT ACTS IN 1904

In the early 1900s, before the invention of television or movies with sound, the most popular form of entertainment was *vaudeville* [VAWD-vil], a kind of "variety" show.

Like Samantha's talent show, a vaude-ville show had many different acts. Performers sang, danced, told jokes, did magic and acrobatic tricks, and showed off trained animals.

Ventriloquists carried on conversations with wooden dummies.

Vaudeville was entertainment for everyone. Theater managers banned words like "slob" and "son of a gun" from the acts so that women and children could attend. Tickets were inexpensive, so middle- and even lower-class people could afford them. And vaudeville houses welcomed people of all nationalities onstage and in the audience.

There were many sister acts in vaudeville.

Some African Americans found success in vaudeville, like comedian Bert Williams. He performed in *blackface*, makeup once worn by white performers to imitate black people. Black performers were required to wear blackface, too, because that was what white audiences expected to see. With his shabby suit and hat and oversized shoes, Williams poked fun not at his own race but at situations that everyone could relate to. He quickly became a star, and he paved the way for other black performers as well.

Vaudeville was a place where women

Offstage, Bert Williams was poised and polished.

were paid as much as, if not more than, men, especially stars like Lillian Russell and Eva Tanguay. Singer Lillian Russell wore expensive, elegant costumes and won over audiences with her voice, beauty, and grace. Eva Tanguay, in contrast, wore outrageous costumes and pranced across the stage as she belted out her songs. She sang and danced so energetically that she was compared to a tornado!

Eva Tanguay

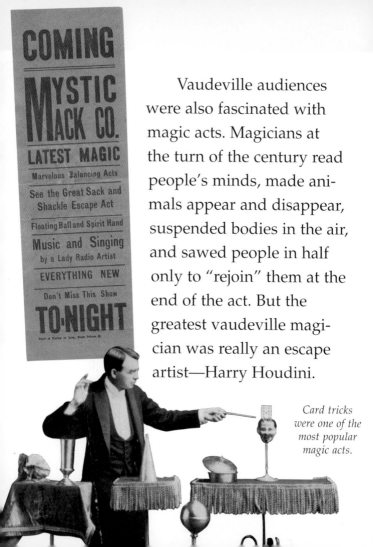

COMING

MYSTIC MACK CO.

LATEST MAGIC

Marvelous Balancing Acts

See the Great Sack and Shackle Escape Act

Floating Ball and Spirit Hand

Music and Singing
by a Lady Radio Artist

EVERYTHING NEW

Don't Miss This Show

TO-NIGHT

Vaudeville audiences were also fascinated with magic acts. Magicians at the turn of the century read people's minds, made animals appear and disappear, suspended bodies in the air, and sawed people in half only to "rejoin" them at the end of the act. But the greatest vaudeville magician was really an escape artist—Harry Houdini.

Card tricks were one of the most popular magic acts.

Houdini could escape from any pair of handcuffs, often in a few minutes or even seconds. He escaped from locked trunks and straitjackets, too. Eventually, he made his escape act more daring by doing it underwater. With his hands chained, Houdini crouched inside a milk can that was filled

Houdini amazed police officers with his "magical" escapes.

with water and locked shut. Several minutes later, a wet and breathless Houdini would emerge from the can— much to the relief of the audience!

Vaudeville greats like Bert Williams, Eva Tanguay, and Harry Houdini inspired many children to enter vaudeville. Some vaudeville houses offered amateur nights, where young performers could test their

Anna and Lillian Roth had an amateur sister act.

talents onstage. On a good night, an amateur act might get the most applause and win a cash prize. On a bad night, an act might disappoint the audience and get "the hook"—a long crooked pole that was used to pull performers right off the stage!

Hooks were long enough to reach performers from either side of the stage.

Comedian Fanny Brice began her vaudeville career in an amateur contest in 1906. When the contestant before her got the hook, someone pushed 14-year-old Fanny onstage. Fanny's act won the contest's five-dollar prize, and she scooped up another five dollars in coins that the appreciative audience had thrown onstage. Fanny started performing in vaudeville houses all over New York City and eventually became one of the most famous female comedians.

"Funny woman" Fanny Brice

Other young stars were born into vaudeville—their parents were performers. These children learned at an early age how to juggle, dance, tell jokes, and sing. Little Buster Keaton joined his mother and father's act almost as soon as he could walk. Carried onstage in a suitcase, the little boy charmed audiences. As a young man, Buster brought his comedy to movies in Hollywood.

The Three Keatons—Buster and his parents

The Palace Theatre was the most famous vaudeville house in America.

Movies eventually brought about the end of vaudeville. The Palace Theatre in New York, where Samantha might have seen vaudeville as a young woman, began showing movies in the early 1930s. Other vaudeville houses followed suit. Sadly, the death of vaudeville meant the end of some of the greatest acts—dancers, singers, and comedians—of all time.

VALERIE TRIPP

At 9   Now

Valerie Tripp says that she became a writer because of the kind of person she is. She says she's curious, and writing requires you to be interested in everything. Talking is her favorite sport, and writing is a way of talking on paper. She's a daydreamer, which helps her come up with her ideas. And she loves words. She even loves the struggle to come up with just the right words as she writes and rewrites. Ms. Tripp lives in Maryland with her husband and daughter.

SARAH MASTERS BUCKEY

At 9   Now

When Sarah Masters Buckey was 14, she got her first job, working as a "page," or aide, at her local library. She loved books, so she enjoyed everything about the job—except having to be quiet!

Ms. Buckey wrote **Samantha's Special Talent**. She is also the author of the History Mysteries titles **Enemy in the Fort** and **The Smuggler's Treasure**. Ms. Buckey lives in New Hampshire with her husband and three children.

DAN ANDREASEN

Dan Andreasen remembers that he always wanted to be an artist. As a child, he copied drawings by Leonardo da Vinci from art books that he checked out of the library. Mr. Andreasen lives in Orlando, Florida, with his wife and three children.